HOP!

PLOP!

Corey Rosen Schwartz & Tali Klein

Illustrations by Olivier Dunrea

WALKER & COMPANY ❋ NEW YORK

Text copyright © 2006 by Corey Rosen Schwartz & Tali Klein
Illustrations copyright © by Olivier Dunrea

First published in the United States of America in 2006 by Walker Publishing Company, Inc.

For information about permission to reproduce selections from this book, write to Permissions, Walker & Company, 175 Fifth Avenue, New York, New York 10010.

Library of Congress Cataloging-in-Publication Data
Schwartz, Corey Rosen.
   Hop! plop! / Corey Rosen Schwartz, Tali Klein ; illustrations by Olivier Dunrea.
      p. cm.
   Summary: When Mouse and Elephant go to the playground together, it seems as if everything they try to play on together is broken, until they finally find the piece of equipment that is just right for them.
   ISBN-10: 0-8027-8056-3 (hardcover)
   ISBN-13: 978-0-8027-8056-0 (hardcover)
   ISBN-10: 0-8027-8057-1 (reinforced)
   ISBN-13: 978-0-8027-8057-7 (reinforced)
   [1. Playgrounds—Fiction. 2. Mice—Fiction. 3. Elephants—Fiction. 4. Best friends—Fiction. 5. Friendship—Fiction.] I. Klein, Tali. II. Dunrea, Olivier, ill. III. Title.
   PZ7.S40715Hop 2006   [E]—dc22   2005027543

Book design by John Candell

The artist used pen-and-ink and gouache on 140-lb. Hot Press Fabriano watercolor paper to create the illustrations for this book.

Visit Walker & Company's Web site at www.walkeryoungreaders.com

Printed in China by South China Printing Company, Dongguan City, Guangdong

2 3 4 5 6 7 8 9 10

FOR DAVID AND YANIV, OUR FAVORITES!

—C. R. S. & T. K.

Mouse yawned.

Elephant yawned.

"I'm bored," said Mouse.

"Me too," sighed Elephant.

"I have an idea," said Mouse.
"Let's go to the playground."

"Great idea!" cried Elephant.

"Look," said Mouse. "A seesaw. My favorite!"

"Yeah!" said Elephant. "Mine too! Let's get on."

HOP!

Mouse climbed back up to the top.

He waited . . .

. . . and he waited.

But the seesaw didn't move.

"I must be too light,"
said Mouse.
"Hmmm. Watermelons
are heavy. Why don't
I eat one?"

"Brilliant idea!" cried Elephant.

So they got a watermelon and . . .

CRUNCH!

SCRUNCH!

SLURP!

MUNCH!

He ate it all up for lunch. (BURP!)

Then Mouse and
Elephant got back
on the seesaw.

SKIP!

TIP!

ZOOM!

ZIP!

Mouse did a backward flip.

"Something is wrong with these seesaws," said Mouse.

"Let's try the swings. They're my favorite."

"Yeah!"
said Elephant.
"Mine too!"

Mouse jumped on.

SWING!

"You try," he said to Elephant. "Maybe you'll have better luck."

PLOP!

DROP!

CRASH!

WHOP!

The swings were
a total flop.

"Let's go on the whirlybird," said Mouse.
"It's my favorite!"

"Yeah!" said Elephant. "Mine too!"

PUSH!

WHOOSH!

ZING!

SMUSH!

Mouse landed
on his tush!

"That does it!" muttered Mouse.
"I'm going home."

"Wait . . . we haven't tried the
slide yet," said Elephant.

"But nothing works! I think this playground is broken," said Mouse.

"I have an idea,"
said Elephant.

"Here's a slide."

"Wow!" Mouse said. He climbed up on Elephant and . . .

"YEEE-OW!"

Mouse's friend beamed with pride.

"Now *that* was fun," Mouse said.
"Elephant, *you* are my favorite!"

"Thanks," said Elephant.
"You're my favorite too."